ALVIN
AND
THE CHIPMUNKS ™

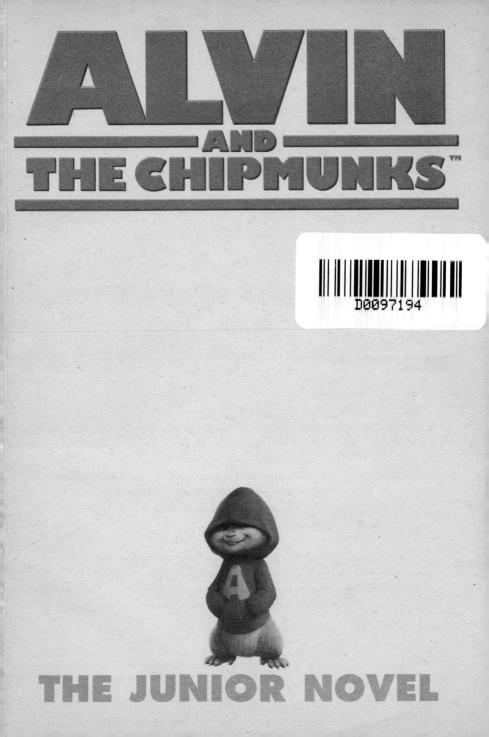

D0097194

THE JUNIOR NOVEL

HarperCollins®, 🍃®, and HarperEntertainment™ are trademarks of HarperCollins Publishers.

Alvin and the Chipmunks: The Junior Novel

Library of Congress catalog card number: 2007934251
ISBN 978-0-06-145064-8

Book design by Sean Boggs

❖

First Edition

ALVIN
AND
THE CHIPMUNKS™

THE JUNIOR NOVEL

Based upon the characters
Alvin and the Chipmunks
created by **Ross Bagdasarian**

Screenplay by **Jon Vitti** and
Will McRobb & Chris Viscardi

Adapted by **Perdita Finn**

HarperEntertainment
An Imprint of HarperCollinsPublishers

chapter 1

The sky was blue and the air was cold. Big fir trees stretched as far as the eye could see in every direction. In the tiny knothole of a huge pine tree, three little chipmunks were working hard. They had to store their nuts away before the full cold blast of winter set in. The weather was already chillier. They sang and chirped and tried not to shiver.

One of the chipmunks, named Alvin, suddenly stopped in mid-song and threw a worm-infested nut down to the ground. He folded his arms and looked out across the forest.

"Alvin, what are you doing?" asked Simon, his brother.

Alvin sighed. "I can't take this anymore!"

Simon, who was the oldest chipmunk, frowned. "Then by all means, stop." Simon paused and glared at Alvin. "I'm sure when you get hungry this winter you can order a pizza."

Theodore staggered over, his little arms full. His cheeks, too, bulged. "A little help, please," he mumbled.

"See, Alvin?" said Simon. "That's how it's done."

"Those are not nuts!" exclaimed Alvin.

"What?" mumbled Theodore, with his mouth full.

Alvin reached out and grabbed one from Theodore and shook his head. "These are rocks. Not nuts."

Alarmed, Theodore spat them out. "I thought they were a little crunchy," he said.

Simon squinted and peered at the little pile at Theodore's feet. "Yup," he said. "Rocks."

In his frustrated mood, Alvin kicked a rock off the branch. "I'm sick of struggling for survival. I'm sick of scratching around in the dirt searching for food." He kicked the branch of the tree he was sitting on. "And I'm especially sick of this stupid, stupid tree!"

The pine tree started to shake when he kicked it. Snow fell from its branches to the ground. But even after Alvin stopped kicking it, the tree kept shaking and a loud whirring noise roared through the forest.

"What's happening?" cried Simon.

"I think Alvin made it angry!" said Theodore, scared.

"What's it gonna do?" said Alvin.

The tree started to teeter, and Alvin clutched Simon and Theodore. *"Whoa!"* screamed all the chipmunks, and they jumped into their knothole at the very last moment. The pine tree, cut down by a chainsaw, toppled to the ground.

The huge fallen tree was quickly wrapped up in plastic netting by men in green jumpsuits. All together, they hoisted the tree up and carried it to a long, red truck already loaded with more firs cut for Christmas. When the tree was finally settled in the truck bed, Alvin poked his head out of the knothole for one last look at the forest. The truck sped away, winding its way down the mountain road, rolling through a tiny town, and finally speeding onto the highway. Skyscrapers loomed in the distance, as the truck rumbled past a billboard that said: WELCOME TO THE CITY OF LOS ANGELES!

chapter 2

Dave Seville was sound asleep in his apartment. But instead of snoozing in his comfy bed, his face was smooshed into his electric keyboard and he was drooling. A couple of guitars stood on stands nearby. Music gear was everywhere, pizza boxes littered the floor, and dirty clothes hung over chairs. Dave shifted in his sleep and accidentally pressed a key. *Blam!* Music from the keyboard burst through the room.

"What? What?" said Dave, startled awake, his dark hair pointing in every direction, a little drool still on his chin. "I'm up. I'm up," he said to himself. Suddenly, he looked at his watch and his eyes opened wide. "And I'm late!"

Dave rushed around the apartment, scrambling to get ready for work. "Okay. Got my jacket," said Dave, going over a mental list. He patted his jacket pocket and felt for his keys. He looked down to make sure his shoes were on his feet. The CD drive on his computer was open. Dave removed a newly burned disk, hunted around on his desk for a pen, and scribbled his name across it. He was headed toward the front door when he stopped, thinking he was forgetting something. What was it? He looked down at his bare legs.

"Pants!" he said aloud. "Need pants. Pants are essential."

Dave grabbed a pair that were hanging over the back of a chair and hopped around the room on one leg trying to get them on as fast as he could. He was still zipping and buttoning as he ran out of his apartment and crashed smack into . . . his ex-girlfriend Claire.

He tried to catch his breath and recover. "How's it going?" he stammered. "I haven't seen you since . . . you said you never wanted to see me again."

Claire, her photography equipment slung over her shoulder, gave him a cool look. "So, I guess it worked," she said.

Dave tried to smooth down his hair. "I remember that. What a fun day that was," he joked.

Claire couldn't help herself. She smiled.

"See? You miss me, don't you?" said Dave, grinning as well.

But Claire wouldn't admit it. She watched as Dave buttoned his pants. "Let me guess," she said. "You're late for something again."

"You're changing the subject," teased Dave. "That means you do miss me."

"Same old Dave," sighed Claire.

"Not following you . . ." said Dave, confused.

"You know," explained Claire. "Dave. The guy who's always joking, who puts his pants on outside, who can't handle a serious relationship."

"That Dave has changed," insisted Dave. "So what do you say we discuss my newfound maturity over dinner?"

Claire looked like she was about to say no, but Dave wouldn't let her. "Tomorrow night? Please? Don't say anything. You look good, Claire." He dashed off toward the parking lot before she could answer him. He'd never make it on time. A little girl on a bike was staring at his car, which was old and beat-up.

"I'm in the early stages of a ten-part restoration process!" explained Dave defensively, as he got inside. "It's a classic." But the little girl didn't buy it. She shook her head and pedaled away.

Dave sped out of the driveway as fast as he could. He just couldn't be late. Not again!

chapter 3

Dave rushed into the office, looking through his pockets and trying to find his tie. Gail, his boss, was standing by her desk, her arms crossed, waiting for him. She was not happy.

"Did you see it?" asked Dave, shaking his head dramatically. "On the news? Huge accident! Total gridlock. A tractor-trailer full of . . . full of . . . monkeys!" He paused for effect. "It was horrible."

"Right," said Gail. Her eyes narrowed. "Do you think, I'm an idiot, Seville? You have a focus group that started ten minutes ago."

Dave tried to look completely cool and relaxed. "I totally knew that," he said. "It's the motor oil thing."

"Good-able Energy Bars," corrected Gail.

"Right!" agreed Dave. "Great product. Totally on top of it." Dave's company tested products to see what real people thought of them before the products went into stores.

"And Mike's out, so you're running it," explained Gail, walking quickly down the hallway.

"No problem," Dave answered. But then he opened the door to the product testing room.

The room was full of kids. Wild, crazy kids. They were running and shouting and bumping into one another. "Good morning, and welcome!" began Dave, and then he backed up, shut the door, and tried to slip away. But Gail was blocking him. She was looking through the two-way mirror at the kids inside.

"They're just kids, Dave," she said sternly. "You don't have to take them home with you."

"Kids? No problem," said Dave, pretending to be calm. "I'm great with kids." He took a deep breath and opened the door again.

"All right, gather around," he announced in a booming voice over the noise. "My name is Dave. And today we want you to taste our new energy bar and tell us what you think." He couldn't believe it. The kids actually quieted down! They were listening to him. Dave picked up an energy bar from the display stand and held it up. "The Good-able Energy Bar . . . ," he began.

A boy grabbed the bar from Dave's hand, tore off the wrapper, took a bite, and spat it out at Dave's feet. "It tastes like poo!" shouted out the boy.

All the kids reacted to what the boy had said and started going wild—laughing and talking to one another and running around the room again. Dave tried to get their attention.

"No! No! No! It doesn't taste like poo!" Dave took a big bite of the bar and quickly turned his back on the kids to spit it out. The kids laughed even louder than ever. They started throwing energy bars at him. "Settle down!" yelled Dave. "I said settle down!" But they weren't listening to him. "AAAH!" screamed Dave, losing it. "YOU LITTLE SPOILED BRATS! WHY CAN'T YOU ACT MORE LIKE GROWN-UPS?"

All the kids froze. The room was completely silent. Then one child started to sniffle. A tear rolled down another little girl's face. Dave knew what was coming next.

"No, don't," he said, trying to make them feel better. "I didn't mean it. I know, let's sing a song!"

But it was too late. All the kids were crying.

Outside in the hallway, Gail, who had been watching through the two-way mirror, dropped her head and let it bang it against the mirror with a big thud.

Later that day in Gail's office, Dave tried to defend himself. "Well, I tasted it, and I gotta tell you, the kid wasn't exactly off target."

Gail frowned at Dave. She didn't have a very good sense of humor. She began lecturing him about the company and about how to get ahead. "There's the power track," she explained, "for the real go-getters. And there's the clock-puncher track for the drones who do only the minimum and are here only to pick up a paycheck. And then there's the track that we don't have a polite name for. We've got big, thick files on them, and we're just waiting for the happy day when a suitable replacement becomes available." Gail seemed pretty clear about what kind of worker she thought Dave was. Still, she asked him, "Exactly what track do you see yourself on, Dave?"

"Uh," hesitated Dave. "Power track?"

"Really?" said Gail, surprised. "I would have lost that bet. Tell me, do you think our clients got their money's worth today?"

"No," said Dave simply. What else *could* he say? Kids were still crying out in the hallway. He checked his watch. Already he was late for his next appointment. "I think we should try again tomorrow."

"Tomorrow?"

"Yeah," said Dave. "In fact, I'm going home right now to work on my presentation. I'm psyched, Gail. I'm totally psyched."

"You're going to another music meeting, aren't you?" Gail was disgusted with him.

"No. No. No," Dave lied.

Gail shook her head. "You know, Dave, I had a dream once. Figure skater. Pretty darn good one, too. But, as I got older, I realized I wasn't good enough."

Dave looked at his watch again. He had to leave now if he was going to make it in time.

"Thankfully, I gave up that dream, and now I run a small company," said Gail, ignoring him. "I am very happy."

Dave stood up and began edging toward the door. "Thanks, Gail. I got a lot out of this." His hand was on the doorknob. "See you bright and early tomorrow!" He dashed out of the room and left the building.

"Your presentation tomorrow better be stellar, pal!" Gail called after him. She sighed and walked over to her desk. She pulled open a drawer and took out an old, worn photo. It was a picture of her as a little girl—dressed in a sparkling figure skater costume.

chapter 4

Dave drove up to the Jett Records Building. He was listening to the CD he'd made of his own music, bopping his head and singing along. Boy, it sounded good! They'd *have* to buy his songs this time.

As he headed into the building to check in at the security desk, he passed an enormous Christmas tree in the lobby. Workers on ladders were stringing up lights and hanging ornaments. Above them, perched on a high branch, were three very surprised little chipmunks.

"Where are we?" whispered Theodore.

"Whoa!" said Alvin, looking around the lobby. "We're in the belly of an alien spacecraft. Those must be the pod people."

Theodore gulped, terrified.

"Give me a break," said Simon. "We're in a building, Theodore."

Meanwhile, Dave was now standing in a special waiting area, surrounded by security guards. A slick, well-dressed man approached him, his arms outstretched. "Dave!" he said, and he gave Dave a quick cool-guy hug. "What's up?" But before Dave could answer, he'd whisked him away toward the elevator. "You ever seen the view from the eightieth floor?" he asked Dave.

"No, Ian." Dave shook his head. "You've never let me get past the lobby."

"Today's your lucky day. You got that song for me?" Ian led him past a gang of hopeful songwriters. As he did, a security guard stepped forward, but Ian brushed him away with a smile and a wave of his hand, "Back off, man. This is Dave Seville. He's with me."

The security guard actually nodded politely. Dave couldn't believe it. This time it was really happening. He was actually going to sell his songs to Jett Records. At last!

"You wanna push the button?" asked Ian, as they got on the elevator.

With a big grin, Dave pressed the button for the eightieth floor. He was going to the top.

Dave leaned back against the elevator wall as it moved upward. He could see it now. He'd be at an awards show, and they'd be announcing his name as the winner of the Best Song of the Year. Dave could see it all in his imagination! A big smile spread across his face as he daydreamed. Just at that moment, the elevator lurched to a halt and the elevator went *ding*. The doors slid open on the eightieth floor.

Sunlight streamed through the floor-to-ceiling windows that offered a spectacular view of the entire city of Los Angeles. Attractive, smiling men and women bustled about the lavish office space.

A beautiful young intern approached Dave. "Can I get you some water, Mr. Seville? Coffee, espresso, soy latte?"

Stunned, Dave barely knew what to say. "Oh, I'd hate to be a bother," he stammered.

"Really, it's no problem," smiled another girl,

appearing at his side.

"How about a muffin? Scone? Pastry?" A third girl held up a huge muffin basket.

Dave's mouth began to water, but all he really wanted was to talk about his music. "No, no, thank you," he said politely.

The double doors to Ian's office automatically opened before him, and together he and Ian walked in. This was it.

As soon as the doors were shut, Ian held up his hand dramatically and Dave gave him the CD of his music. Ian slipped it into a CD player and took a seat behind his desk. The music began to play. Dave looked at Ian expectantly.

"Dave," Ian leaned over and hit the pause button on the CD player. "Let's talk about your song."

Dave was so excited, he could barely stand it. The words came tumbling out. "Well, as crazy as it sounds, the original inspiration came to me—"

"The song sucks, Dave," interrupted Ian.

There was a long pause. "Uh . . . what?" asked Dave

finally. He wasn't sure he'd heard Ian correctly.

"Your song. It's awful. I hate it. Who's going to sing this? I need new, Dave. Fresh. The next big thing." Ian patted Dave on the shoulder and quickly removed his hand, an expression of disgust on his face. He casually pumped some hand sanitizer onto his hands to get the germs off. "We go way back, Dave. We've both come a long way from college. Well, you not so much. And if I weren't your friend, I'd tell you to keep reaching for the stars, blah, blah, blah. But I *am* your friend, and there's no point of writing songs that no one is ever, ever going to sing."

Dave was dumbfounded. This was not what he'd expected to hear.

"I'd hate to see you wind up as one of those thirty-five-year-old guys hanging around the lobby," said Ian.

"I'm thirty-six," said Dave.

"Case in point," said Ian.

In a daze, Dave wandered out of Ian's office. He felt as if he'd been punched in the stomach. No one in the outer office would look him in the eye when he came out. He shuffled over to one of the pretty girls who'd approached him when he first came in. "You know, that water sounds pretty good right about now."

"We ran out," she replied without even looking up.

Dave looked at the muffin basket and reached out for one, but another girl slid them away from him. Dave got the message. He started to head toward the elevator, but just as the doors opened to take him back down to the lobby, he darted back, grabbed the entire basket of muffins, hugged it to his chest, and made a run for it.

"Hey!" shouted the intern.

But the doors of the elevator slid shut. Dave and the muffin basket were gone.

chapter 5

Alvin had climbed down the Christmas tree and was standing on the floor of the lobby. "C'mon!" he called to his brothers. Simon scurried after him, but Theodore was frightened. Nervously, he looked around, still holding on to a last branch until Simon came back and pulled him away from the tree.

The lobby was full of dangers! Which way should they go? An enormous hand truck veered toward them. Yikes! As they jumped in the other direction, a mail carrier zoomed past with his cart.

"Hey, watch it!" said Dave, who was rushing through the lobby on his way home. He stepped aside to avoid being hit. As he struggled to regain his balance, a muffin fell out of his basket—right in front of the chip-munks. The mail carrier veered around them.

They looked up at Dave in awe. If he hadn't stepped in front of them, they would have been run over.

"He saved us!" said Simon.

"He fed us!" said Theodore, looking at the enormous muffin.

"He's getting away!" noticed Alvin. With a huge leap, Alvin hurled himself into Dave's muffin basket. Simon followed, and a second later, Theodore did the same. He nearly didn't make it, but Simon grabbed him by the scruff of his neck at the last minute. Whew! They were all safe.

"Has anyone tried the chocolate chip?" asked Theodore a few minutes later.

"*Ssh!* Theodore!" whispered Simon.

"Maybe he lives in a nice, cozy home," said Theodore, who was looking up at the man carrying the basket.

"Quiet!" commanded Simon. They couldn't risk being found out. Not yet, anyway.

They were on the road again. But where were they going this time?

chapter 6

Dave felt terrible. As he entered his apartment, he looked down at the basket of muffins. He didn't even know why he'd taken it. He walked into the kitchen, dropped the entire basket into the garbage can, and closed the lid.

Carefully, a little chipmunk poked his head out of the basket. "His house isn't as cozy as I thought," said Theodore in the dark.

"I believe we're in the garbage," explained Simon.

Back in the living room, Dave was staring at all his music gear. It sickened him. He marched over to the keyboard, yanked out the power cord, and chucked the keyboard out the front door into the courtyard.

The rest of the gear followed.

Finally, the only thing left of his musical career was a poster on the wall. He peeled off the poster and rehung it, this time facing the wall.

In the kitchen, the chipmunks lifted the lid of the garbage can and poked out their heads. Simon counted to three, and Alvin hopped onto the counter. Theodore and Simon followed.

"Let's see what he's got," said Alvin, examining the cupboard. After their long rides, first in the truck and then in Dave's car, he was hungry. He tapped on the cabinets with his paws, listening like a safe cracking bank robber for what was inside. Finally, he yanked open a door. He'd hit pay dirt! On the shelves were boxes of cereal, popcorn, snacks, bags of chips—the mother lode!

"*Woooowwww!*" squealed all the chipmunks together.

"This must be where he stores his food for winter," said Simon, amazed.

In an instant, Theodore had climbed up into the cabinet, knocked over a box of sugared cereal, and climbed completely inside. "This is the greatest day of my life!" he yelled to the others.

Alvin tipped over a bag of white cheddar cheese balls, and, miraculously, it emptied right into a bowl that was already on the counter.

"Who wants cheese balls?" he asked, grinning. Then he raised his arms and dived headfirst into the bowl!

"Don't open anything!" Simon was worried. "Don't make a mess," he pleaded. He was listening to the sounds from the other room. "He's coming! *Hide!*" He ducked behind the cereal box where Theodore was still munching. Alvin scrambled under the cheese balls.

Dave couldn't believe the mess when he came into the kitchen—cabinets open, boxes spilling out onto the counter. He shook his head. "I don't remember leaving those open," he said aloud. He walked over and shut the cabinets and was just heading back to the living room when he heard a noise. A tiny noise. He listened, shrugged, and left the room. But then he heard it again. A high-pitched whispering, some shuffling. It sounded like someone was in the kitchen. Dave poked his head back through the kitchen door.

Three jumbo coffee mugs were sitting on the countertop. For a moment, it had seemed to Dave as if they were moving, but no, now they were absolutely still. How could they move on their own anyway? Nobody was in the kitchen. But as he released the door, he heard it again, more whispering and skittering. This time, he decided to be bold. He grabbed his spatula and raised it above his head. He swatted at the coffee cups, and they shattered across the counter. Nothing was inside them, though. They were completely empty.

Dave looked around the counter. A bowl was overflowing with cheese balls. He hadn't done that. A bag of tortilla chips was torn open. He hadn't done that either. He heard a rustling noise and saw a small furry tail emerging from the bag. Out came Theodore, several large chips in his mouth.

Theodore looked up and saw Dave. He froze. Dave raised his spatula and let out a war cry.

"No!" screamed Alvin, and he hurled himself at Dave's face.

Simon grabbed the light switch and turned it off, plunging the room into darkness. Dave crashed into the table as he struggled to find the switch. He got the lights back on, but the animals were gone. Where were they? He began searching the apartment.

Suddenly, Dave stopped and looked. In the corner of the living room mirror, he just made out Alvin—clinging to the back of his head by his hair. Pretending not to notice, Dave carefully made his way to the front door of his apartment, grabbed a winter hat from a peg on the wall, and jammed it on his head. "Now I've got you!" Dave yelled.

But his triumph quickly became pain as the little chipmunk thrashed around inside the hat. Dave whipped it off and slammed it on the table. Dave caught his breath and peeked under the hat. Out came Alvin's paw and slapped Dave across the face twice. Alvin bolted out of the hat and back into the kitchen.

Dave rushed after him and just managed to see a chipmunk tail disappearing into the cookie jar. Carefully, Dave sneaked closer. "I might as well go to bed," he said loudly. "It's not like there's anything here I want . . . to CAPTURE."

Dave grabbed the cookie jar and started shaking it over his head and doing a victory dance. But then he saw that the window was open. Had they escaped?

"I thought I closed that," said Dave. He walked over to the window, and as he passed the cabinets, another jar tipped over and smashed onto his head. The room was spinning, spinning, spinning. And then it went black.

chapter 7

"I think you killed him," said Theodore, standing over Dave.

Alvin looked around frantically, worried. "Let's get out of here. Wipe everything down."

"Shouldn't we call an ambulance?" asked Simon.

Dave's eyelids fluttered. He was coming to. "I must be hearing things," he muttered.

Theodore bent over his face. "Are you all . . . ," but before he could say anything else, Alvin had slapped his hand over his mouth.

Dave's eyes widened in disbelief. He stared at the chipmunks. The chipmunks stared at Dave, absolutely frozen. Finally, Dave chuckled. Of course, he'd been imagining things. "Whoa. That was trippy," he said out loud, shaking his head.

"Tell me about it," sighed Alvin with relief.

Dave screamed and scrambled away from the chipmunks as fast as he could. "Get back!" he yelled at them. He was freaked out. "SQUIRRELS CAN'T TALK!"

"Hey, hey, watch it pal!" said Alvin, offended. "We're *chipmunks*."

"Chipmunks can't talk either!" yelled Dave.

Simon shrugged. "We disagree."

"This isn't happening," said Dave. He closed his eyes, willing the chipmunks to disappear. When he opened his eyes, they would all be gone. Only they weren't. "I am not talking to chipmunks, I am not talking to chipmunks," he repeated to himself.

"Hate to burst your bubble, Dave," said Alvin.

"How do you know my name?"

"Let's see. Your mail, your wallet . . . ," explained Alvin.

"Alvin, give him back his wallet," scolded Simon.

Dave rubbed his eyes. It had been a hard day. It really had, but he certainly didn't feel crazy. "Can *all* animals talk?" he asked.

The chipmunks were disgusted by the question. "They're *animals*, Dave," said Simon.

"Do you want to know if cars can talk? 'Cause here's a hint. They can't," said Alvin.

Dave gave Alvin a dirty look. Simon laughed uncomfortably.

"We're getting off on the wrong foot," interrupted Simon. "Allow us to introduce ourselves. I'm Simon, and this is Alvin."

" 'S'up playa?" said Alvin, trying to be cool.

"And I'm Theodore!" chirped Theodore, interrupting.

"Nice to meet you," said Dave. "Now get out of my house."

Immediately, all three chipmunks looked crushed. They'd begun to like Dave. And they really liked his cereal. "But we can talk," pleaded Theodore.

Dave was firm. "The fact that you can talk only makes me want you out of my house that much more. It's creepy. Unnatural. Somewhat evil."

"We liked you better when you were unconscious . . . ,"

Alvin said. Before Alvin knew what was happening, Dave grabbed a wicker basket and slammed it over all the chipmunks. *Wham!*

"Gotcha!" said Dave. He slid a cookie sheet under the basket, trapping all three chipmunks inside.

After Dave dumped them outside, the chipmunks managed to climb up the apartment building to Dave's window ledge. It wasn't any harder to climb than a pine tree, really. They peeked in through the window, heartbroken expressions on their little faces. Dave was cleaning up the mess in the kitchen.

"Shoo! Leave me alone," yelled Dave when he saw them. He yanked down the shade.

The chipmunks looked sad. They went back to the door of the apartment building and sat on the front steps without saying a word. Later, Dave came out, carrying the rest of his music equipment. He stacked it up by the garbage cans. The chipmunks pretended to shiver in the cool night air. Dave didn't even acknowledge them—he just stepped right over them each time.

Dave went in and swept out the rest of his music room. It felt good to have all that music equipment gone. This was the beginning of the new Dave. The responsible Dave. It felt good to think about growing up at last. He could hear it beginning to rain outside.

From out in the rain, he heard the saddest of songs being sung in beautiful three-part harmony. Dave stopped his sweeping for a moment to listen. "No way," he said to himself, as he threw open the window. The three chipmunks were huddled together on the ledge. They stopped their singing when they saw him.

"Feel bad now, Dave?" asked Alvin.

"This is officially blowing my mind. You can sing, too?"

"Tip of the iceberg, Dave," said Alvin.

Hoping to impress Dave, the chipmunks launched into a funky and funny song with cool dance moves. *It's the next big thing*, thought Dave. "This is amazing," he said out loud. He peered around outside to make sure no one was watching. "Everyone inside."

Theodore rushed in, followed by Alvin. But Simon

smacked into the window frame. He couldn't see very well. Dave looked at him curiously and helped him to his feet. Then he closed the window.

"Perhaps I was a little hasty," said Dave. "I think we can work something out. If you sing my songs, you get to sleep here."

"Does breakfast come with that?" piped up Theodore.

"Done. But don't tell your animal friends about this. I don't want to come home to find a bunch of rabbits and skunks on the couch."

"We don't have any friends," said Simon seriously.

"Except you!" chirped Theodore.

"Let's not get ahead of ourselves," said Dave. "I'm not your friend. I'm your songwriter."

Alvin was surprised. "You're gonna write songs for us?"

"Yes," said Dave. He walked over to his keyboard . . . except it wasn't there. "Oh, man!" He ran out into the rain to rescue his equipment from the garbage. It was time to be a songwriter again!

chapter 8

Dave was sitting at his keyboard, ready for a night of music. "So all we've got to do," he explained to the chipmunks, "is find the right song, rehearse it, and . . ." But the chipmunks weren't paying any attention to him. They were much more interested in exploring his apartment. Simon had found a piece of paper and made a paper airplane. He tossed it into the air, and it soared across the room, making little loops as it flew.

"Simon!" said Dave, coming into the room. "You're going to break something with that." He reached out his hand to grab the plane and saw Alvin twirling a ring around his waist. "Alvin. That's not a hula hoop. It's a napkin ring."

"Are you guys always like this?" Dave asked.

"We're kids, Dave," explained Simon.

"Then where're your parents?" asked Dave.

"When you're a chipmunk, your parents take care of you for a week, and then they take off," answered Simon.

"Ours left early," added Alvin.

Just at that moment, Dave noticed Theodore on a nearby shelf. He was being chased by an old-fashioned windup Santa Claus toy. "Theodore, be careful," cried Dave, exasperated.

Theodore slipped and fell. Dave lunged but managed to catch only the Santa Claus. Theodore hit the couch and bounced toward the ceiling.

"Sorry!" he squeaked.

Carefully, Dave put the toy back on the shelf. "That's a collectible," he scolded Theodore. "I got it for Christmas last year."

All the chipmunks stopped and stared at Dave. "Christmas!" they yelled together.

"We love Christmas!" said Alvin.

Recovering from his excitement, Simon explained, "Even though we've never actually celebrated it."

"But we want to!" squealed Theodore.

"Can't go wrong with Christmas," agreed Dave.

"Maybe we can celebrate it with you," said Theodore shyly.

"Uh, yeah, maybc," said Dave uncomfortably. "Look, guys, I've had a long and weird day, so off to bed. We start work tomorrow. I want you bright-eyed and bushy-tailed by eight."

"My tail isn't bushy until nine," said Alvin.

"Not my problem," said Dave. "Now off to bed." Dave switched off the living room light. He paused at his bedroom door, listening to the chipmunks chatter. Even their speaking voices were musical.

"I hope Christmas comes fast," said Alvin.

"Me, too!" said Theodore.

The chipmunks snuggled up together and were soon fast asleep. Alvin started snoring, then Theodore, and finally Simon. Their snores made a little melody. It was a kind of catchy tune, really. And as he lay in bed, Dave found himself humming it. He couldn't get it out of his head. He mumbled some words, and they fit. He sat bolt upright in bed. That was it! He had a song!

All night long, Dave worked at his keyboard, listening through his headphones and making notes as he went. He was so excited to be writing a brand-new song. Eventually, he went to get his guitar to add its sound to the mix, and he passed the chipmunks cuddled up asleep on the couch.

When he was finally done with the song, Dave got glue, cardboard, and scissors and made a Christmas diorama. He added a hula hoop and a looping airplane to the scene. He yawned. He was tired. He'd just rest his head on the keyboard for a minute.

The first light of dawn was breaking over the city.

Dave was jarred awake by the sound of the television blasting from the living room.

He staggered into the kitchen and discovered that once again it was a disaster area. The chipmunks had been cooking breakfast.

Theodore was standing next to a carton of frozen

toaster waffles, and Simon was beside a timer. The buzzer went off just as Dave walked into the room. Smoke was pouring out of the toaster.

"Evacuate the waffle!" screamed Simon.

"Fire in the hole! Fire in the hole!" yelled Alvin.

"What in the . . . ," began Dave, but he was interrupted by a burned waffle flying through the air.

"I got it! I got it!" yelled Simon. The waffle landed on the counter, three feet away from him.

"Where'd it go?" asked Simon, whirling around.

Dave studied Simon. There was something wrong with this chipmunk, and he thought he knew what it was. "Simon, how many fingers am I holding up?" he asked. Dave wasn't holding up any fingers at all.

Simon squinted. "Somewhere between four and eight," he guessed.

Dave went into the other room and came back with a tiny pair of glasses from one of his toys on the shelf. "Try these," he said. He slid the glasses onto Simon's face.

"Wow!" said Simon, looking around. "This place is a pigsty!"

Dave had to smile, but then he became stern again. "It wasn't when I went to bed last night."

"I begged them to behave," sighed Simon. "But there's only so much I can do."

"We colored for a long time," said Theodore. "Then we got hungry. Want to see what we colored?"

"No," answered Dave. "Just sit down. I wrote a song for you guys to sing to a . . . " Dave stopped. He noticed a bump under the carpet. "Did you guys hide something under my rug?"

Alvin looked a little embarrassed. "We put a few toaster waffles aside for winter."

Dave lifted up a corner of the carpet and looked at the syrup-covered waffles. He shook his head. Chipmunks were a lot of work! "Okay, guys, there's going to be food all winter," he reassured them. "If you start storing it, it's gonna get gross and we're gonna have . . ." Dave stopped in mid-sentence. He realized he had been just about to make a terrible mistake. He'd been going to say "rodents," but weren't chipmunks rodents, too? He already had rodents! "Um," he tried

40

again. "We're gonna have bad non-talking rodents here."

The chipmunks scrunched up their faces! Non-talking rodents! Yuck!

"Anyway," continued Dave, "here's how the song goes." He sat down at the keyboard and began playing and singing the brand-new Christmas song he had written the night before. He forgot about everything that had happened since he woke up, and watched the chipmunks' faces. They were all smiling. He knew it. It was a great song. Their little voices joined with his.

Across the courtyard, Claire was headed out on an assignment with her camera equipment slung over her shoulder. As she headed to her car, she stopped for a moment. She could hear the music coming from Dave's apartment.

What an endearing, offbeat song! she thought. It had to be Dave. She had always liked his songs. She smiled in spite of herself.

chapter 9

Dave set the portable stereo down on Ian's desk. Somehow, he had managed to make it back up to the eightieth floor of Jett Records—only this time the chipmunks were with him. He placed a larger box on the floor next to the desk.

"Ian, this is it. I've got your next big thing." He was barely able to contain his excitement.

Ian shook his head sadly. "Dave, don't do this to yourself," he pleaded.

"I'm not asking you. I'm telling you. Watch."

Dave hit the play button. The intro music to the chipmunks' Christmas song began to play. After only a few notes, Dave whipped off the cover of the other box and revealed the chipmunks themselves on a miniature stage—the one Dave had made just a few days before out of glue and cardboard.

Ian was surprised. This was actually pretty interesting. At the very least, it was unusual. Dave put his arm around Ian with a big smile of anticipation. This was the moment when dreams come true, he thought. This was the moment when he, Dave Seville, would become a famous songwriter. He listened to the music. It was just about time for the chipmunks to begin singing. Almost. Almost. Now!

But the chipmunks didn't sing. They stood in front of the painted winter scene completely frozen with fear. Their mouths were open, but no sound was coming out.

Slowly, Dave's smile faded. He gestured to the boys, trying to encourage them to join in. But they didn't move. They didn't sing. They may as well have been little stuffed toys. Dave turned to Ian to try to explain. "They sing," he said.

Ian stared at the chipmunks for another moment and

then turned back to Dave. "No," he said. "They don't."

Dave tried to prompt them. "Come on!" he urged. He hummed a little. He sang a few bars of the song himself. *"Me, I want a hula hoop."*

"Kinda weird for a grown man to want a hula hoop, Dave," said Ian.

"I'm not gonna sing it," Dave warned the chipmunks.

"Who would then?" asked Ian. "Nobody's gonna touch something this nice."

"No! I told you," I said Dave. "They're gonna sing it!"

Ian stared at the chipmunks. Theodore scratched his ear with his hind leg.

For a long time, Dave drove without saying anything. The chipmunks were beside him in the passenger seat. Finally, he couldn't help asking.

"What happened?" he demanded.

"He was throwing out some weird vibes," said Theodore.

"Yeah, why do we have to sing for him, anyway?" asked Alvin.

"How's this?" said Dave. "Pretend I need the money and I hate my job and you're staying at my place so you owe me."

"We're sorry," said Theodore, trembling. He reached out and put his paw on Dave's arm.

"Yeah, that helps," said Dave bitterly. He sighed. So much for dreams. "Never mind. I'm late for work."

"Can we go with you?" chirped Theodore.

"What? So you can mess that up, too? Nope. You're going home."

The chipmunks didn't know what to say. Alvin watched Dave as he drove along the highway. He couldn't resist. "Can I beep the horn?" he begged.

Dave glared at him.

chapter 10

Dave arrived to work on time in a suit. He looked very sharp. He was carrying professional presentation boards, but he looked frazzled. Gail barely noticed his new look. She was glancing at her watch. "The clients are waiting, Dave."

She led him down the hall and opened the door to the conference room. It was time for Dave to show the Good-able Energy Bar clients his ideas for advertisements. The three clients—Ted, Amy, and Barry—were sitting at the table while Dave set up his presentation.

"Hey, guys," began Dave. "I'm really jazzed about our Yum-able Energy Bars commercial . . ."

"Good-able," corrected Gail, through gritted teeth.

"Right!" said Dave. He launched into a description of the commercial he wanted to put on television. "We open up on a group of tired-looking kids. Close up on a little girl. She's sad."

Barry frowned. "I don't like that she's sad."

Ted agreed. "Our customers don't like to think of their kids as being sad."

"Could she be flying a kite?" Gail suggested.

Ted, Amy, and Barry all nodded to one another. They liked that idea! Gail was good at this! They turned back to Dave.

He took a deep breath and continued. "Great! She's flying a kite. She's running with the kite." He was trying to imagine what would happen in this new commercial. He got up and started acting it out. He was running around the table holding an imaginary kite. Then he began to gasp for breath. "Now, she's running out of steam," he explained.

The clients looked at one another and nodded. Even Gail seemed to like this idea.

"She's tired," said Dave. "And she lets go of her kite.

Oh, no! We see her face. It's sad."

"But not *too* sad," interrupted Amy.

"Right!" agreed Dave. "Point being, she wants her kite, but it's getting away. She pulls out her Good-able Energy Bar and . . ." But before he could go any further, he was interrupted by a cell phone. His cell phone. Gail and the clients frowned again.

"Uh, sorry," said Dave. "It's my mom. Hello?"

"Little situation," a little voice squealed through the receiver. "Theodore vacuumed up Alvin!"

"WHAT?" screamed Dave into the receiver.

"Alvin's in the vacuum!" said Simon again. "Oh, no! There goes Theodore, too!"

Completely embarrassed, Dave tried to cover up. "I can't do this right now." He held up his finger to the clients as if to say he'd be back in just a second.

"I absolutely understand," said Simon, trying to be reasonable. "But the sink is overflowing and . . ."

"If you flood my house, you are dead! Like out on the street, *capische*?!" yelled Dave.

The clients glanced at one another, frightened. Dave

seemed a little unstable.

Dave snapped shut his cell phone and put it away. He smiled nervously at the clients.

"Mothers," he said. "Anyway, the girl gets her kite back. Now I have some impressive sales projections aimed directly at the youth market."

Dave went over to an easel where he had placed his presentation boards. He had spent a lot of time creating them. "When I first saw these, I didn't think it could be true, but I looked again . . ." Dave flipped over a page to reveal a very professional graph showing how his commercial would improve sales of the energy bars. But scrawled across it in Magic Marker were the words "Size of Theodore's Butt."

Dave couldn't believe it. "We'll come back to that!" He stepped in front of the easel and tried to distract the clients. He continued speaking. "Ten years ago, the market share of healthy food snacks was imperceptible among six- to twelve-year-olds." He was talking as fast as he could, hoping that the clients hadn't seen the graffiti on the graph.

He flipped to a new graph. A big colored line soared upward. Written above it in childish print were the words "How Much Alvin Smells."

Dave felt ill. He quickly flipped to the next page, which showed a pair of bar graphs—only the original words had been crossed out and replaced. Under the first one were the words "How Smart Simon Thinks He Is," and under the other, "How Smart He Actually Is."

Dave peeked at the next card and groaned. "I'm not even going to show you that one," he said.

None of the Good-able Energy Bar clients said anything. Gail didn't say anything. They all just stared at Dave. Finally, Dave broke the silence. "So, are there any questions?"

Amy, one of the clients, raised her hand. "What makes Alvin so smelly?"

Gail glared at Dave.

Dave looked sheepish. So much for the power track. "I should just clean out my office."

Gail didn't disagree with him. Dave was fired.

chapter 11

The front door flew open, and Dave burst into the apartment, his presentation boards under one arm and a banker's lockbox in the other. "What is this about?" he screamed, holding up the boards covered in graffiti.

Theodore blinked nervously. "We told you we colored."

"On my presentation boards?" yelled Dave. "You got me fired."

Poor Theodore. He felt just terrible. He could hardly look at Dave. "We didn't know," he stammered. "We're sorry, Dave." He really was.

"You're sorry? Oh, that's fantastic! 'Sorry' doesn't get my job back, now does it, Theodore?" He stopped in mid-rant when he noticed the apartment. This was all too much for him. He wasn't up to chipmunks. "Why are my clothes all over the place?"

Simon rushed forward to explain. "We used them to mop up the floor."

"Oh my goodness! Theodore!" exclaimed Dave. "Did you just . . ." Next to Theodore was a dark, round pellet.

"It's a raisin, Dave!" Simon said, trying to reassure him.

Dave wasn't so sure. "Prove it," he said.

Simon took a big breath and bit the pellet. Staring at Dave the whole time, he chewed and chewed and, finally, swallowed.

But Dave was still angry. He called all the chipmunks to come together—but Alvin was nowhere to be found. Dave stormed into the kitchen looking for him.

"You owe me big-time!" whispered Simon to Theodore after Dave had left the room.

In the kitchen, Dave was throwing open cabinet doors and lifting the lids off jars in his hunt for Alvin. "ALLLLLVIN!" he shouted again and again in his fury.

Where could he be? Dave stopped finally and listened. From the humming dishwasher came another, higher-pitched, sound—the sound of a singing chipmunk. Dave yanked open the dishwasher door, and sure enough, there was Alvin, covered in soap.

"Someone's in here!" said Alvin, trying to cover himself up.

"Get out," demanded Dave.

"I'm waiting for the rinse cycle," pleaded Alvin.

"Out!"

Dave was ranting. "If I made a list of my worst days ever, guess what? Today would be at the top of the list!"

"The day is still young," said Alvin. "You can turn it around."

"Clam it, sudsy!" shouted Dave. As Alvin exited the dishwasher, an embarrassed Theodore and Simon slunk across the kitchen counter. Accidentally, Theodore stepped on the answering machine.

Dave was still raging when the machine beeped. *"Hi, Dave,"* played the message. *"It's Claire Wilson calling. Why did I just say my last name? That was weird. Um, I guess I'm just a little nervous about coming over for dinner . . ."*

"Dinner!" shrieked Dave. In all the chaos, he'd forgotten about it.

"So, I'm just going to hang up now," continued Claire's voice on the answering machine. *"I'll be there at seven, okay? Bye."*

Dave jerked his head and looked at the clock on the wall. It was already 6:30. "That's half an hour," said Dave to himself.

The chipmunks had all crowded around when they heard the lady's voice coming out of the answering machine. "Who's Claire?" giggled Theodore.

"Claire is Dave's mate," said Simon.

"She's not my 'mate,'" disagreed Dave. "She's my . . . ex-mate."

All the chipmunks giggled mischievously. "Do you love her?" asked Simon.

"It's none of your business," snapped Dave. He scrambled to start cleaning up the apartment.

"He loves her!" giggled the chipmunks.

"I can't believe this," said Dave, looking around at the mess.

"Dave, you go," said Simon reassuringly. "We've got thirty minutes. You get the food, and we'll take care of the rest."

"Why don't I believe you?" asked Dave.

"Have faith, Dave," said Alvin.

"We're all in this together," said Simon.

"Like a family!" chirped Theodore.

"No!" Dave disagreed. "Not like a family."

"Tick-tock, Dave," said Alvin, pointing to the clock. "Better get moving."

Dave peered around the room one last time. He had no choice. He had to trust them. He sprinted out the front door to grab something to eat for dinner.

When he returned with takeout food, the apartment was amazingly clean. Except it smelled funny. "What is that?" asked Dave.

"Your cologne," said Alvin. "Manly, no?"

"What did you do? Dump the whole bottle on the rug?"

"We call it scenting the area," explained Simon.

Dave carried his food into the kitchen. It, too, was

sparkling. "I got to admit it," he said. "I'm surprised. The place looks great."

"We chipmunks are a notoriously tidy species," said Simon proudly.

Dave was impressed—until he opened the refrigerator. It was crammed full of laundry, a skateboard, and all kinds of disgusting garbage. "Yeah," said Dave, shaking his head. "I can see that. So where'd you get the flowers?"

"Here and there," answered Alvin vaguely.

Dave couldn't see that all the neighbors' flower bushes had been pruned.

Back in the living room, Dave discovered the dining room table set for five. "Guys," said Dave. "I don't know how to tell you this, but it's just gonna be Claire and me tonight."

Alvin's face fell. "You mean we can't . . ."

"No," said Dave at once.

"Even if . . . ," asked Simon.

"No," said Dave again.

"You won't even know we're . . ."

"And no . . . ," Dave said as he herded them toward his bedroom and shut the door. He took a deep breath. He'd missed Claire so much. He couldn't believe they were finally having dinner again together.

Dave Seville is a songwriter with a dream.

He was down
        on his luck . . .

. . . until he met some very special chip.

Dave meets with Ian, an executive at Jett Records.

Ian is impressed.

These are no ordinary rodents!

Dave hears a familiar song on the radio—his song.

Meet the
worlds biggest
rock stars:

ALVIN, SIMON, and THEODORE!

Dave makes a sad discovery—
the chipmunks have left.

Dave looks for them at the concert,
but finds Ian instead.

Will the chipmunks come back home,
or is "Uncle Ian" their new family?

chapter 12

Claire put her fork down on her plate and gazed at Dave. "I had no idea you could cook like this." She was stunned.

Dave tried to appear nonchalant. "It's all about slow-roasting. It takes more time, but when it comes to flavor, why rush?"

"I'm impressed."

The tiny faces of three chipmunks peeked out from behind the bedroom door.

"How do you think it's going?" whispered Theodore. Dave and Claire were eating again.

"Terrible!" said Alvin. "They're not even sniffing each other." Alvin ventured out of the bedroom.

"Don't go out there!" ordered Simon. "Dave said . . ." But it was too late.

Dave was asking Claire about her work. "I've been seeing your photographs in the paper."

"Yeah," answered Claire. "It's going great. They really seem to like my stuff. How about you? How's your job?"

Dave choked for a moment, swallowed, recovered, and lied. "Loving it."

Claire was just telling Dave how nice it was to be hanging out together again when the stereo blasted on with a steamy pop hit. Her fork suspended in midair, Claire looked around, wondering who had turned on the music.

"Oh, the stereo does that all the time." Dave thought fast. "It's like it has a mind of its own. Um, you were saying?"

"I was nervous coming here. I wasn't sure if you thought this was, like, a date or something."

"A date?" said Dave, pretending to be surprised. "No. No."

At that moment, the lights dimmed romantically.

"Huh?" Dave was startled. "It's these old buildings. The wiring is shot," he said, glancing around, trying to figure out where the chipmunks were hiding.

"You should have an electrician fix it," said Claire.

But Dave wasn't listening to her. He was looking for the chipmunks. He shouted so that they would hear him wherever they were. "I DON'T NEED ANYONE TO FIX ANYTHING FOR ME!"

"OKAY!" yelled Claire in response.

"Could you excuse me for a moment?" asked Dave, agitated. "I'm going to check the fuse box." He hurried into the bedroom. When the door was firmly shut behind him, he cornered Simon and Theodore. "I know what you guys are up to! Where's Alvin?" He glanced around the room. "Alvin?"

After smelling Dave's breath, Theodore found the breath spray and grabbed it. He blasted it toward Dave's mouth—and missed. The spray hit Dave smack in the eye.

"OW!" wailed Dave. He staggered backward,

knocking things over and making a huge *CRASH!*

"Dave, are you okay?" shouted Claire from the next room.

"Everything's fine!" responded Dave. He clutched his burning eye. "Why did you do that?" asked Dave.

"You have garlic breath," said Theodore. "I was just trying to help."

Dave grabbed the breath spray and hurled it against the wall. "Well, stop helping. You're ruining everything," he whispered. He stormed out of the bedroom and tried to compose himself. His eye still hurt, and he rubbed it.

"Sorry," he said to Claire. "I guess I got something in my eye."

"Let me see," said Claire, getting up.

She peered into Dave's blurry eye. Behind her, Dave saw Alvin by the couch. Dave reached toward the table, grabbed a roll, and whipped it at Alvin. It crashed. He'd missed.

Claire spun around at the sudden noise. "What was that?"

"I have rats," said Dave.

Alvin popped out of his hiding place. He was furious. He was not a rat.

"Tomorrow I'm calling an exterminator," said Dave.

Alvin picked up the roll and threw it with all his might. It smacked Dave on the side of his head.

"OW!" he wailed again. He staggered and tripped. Claire turned to look around. To keep her from seeing Alvin, Dave grabbed her and hugged her awkwardly. He waved at Alvin to get out of sight.

"Dave!" cried Claire, startled. "What are you doing?" She pushed him away and got to her feet as quickly as she could.

"Sorry!" Dave was so embarrassed. What a day it had been! And things just kept getting worse and worse. He had to tell Claire. "I lost my job today," he admitted. "And I guess what I really needed was a hug."

"That was a weird hug," said Claire.

"Sorry. Maybe what I really need is someone to talk to."

Claire's face softened. "Why didn't you just say so? Tell me what happened, Dave."

Dave hesitated. Should he tell her the *whole* story? The evening had been going so well. And he missed Claire. He needed her, especially now. "This is going to sound a little strange," he began.

"No jokes," said Claire. "No fooling around."

Dave took a deep breath. "The truth?"

"Please, Dave," insisted Claire. "I'm begging you."

Dave waited for a moment, trying to think of some way to explain everything in a way that didn't make him sound crazy. But he couldn't. He just had to tell her. "My life is being sabotaged by talking chipmunks."

That was it. Claire didn't hesitate. She bolted from the table and out the front door like it was a fire drill.

"Don't go," Dave pleaded. "I can explain! Claire!"

But it was too late. Claire was gone.

chapter 13

Dave collapsed on his bed and covered his eyes with his arms. It had all been too horrible. He'd told Claire he'd lost his job. He'd told her about the chipmunks. Now she not only thought he was a loser, but she thought he was crazy, too.

The chipmunks were very worried. They called to Dave from the living room. "Please come out! It's gonna be okay."

"Go away!" Dave yelled. "Leave me alone."

Nestled together on the foldout couch, the chipmunks talked about it.

"That went nicely," said Simon sarcastically.

"He really did have garlic breath," said Theodore.

"We have to do something," said Simon.

"I know what we can do," said Alvin. He had a plan.

In his bedroom, Dave was realizing the chipmunks were too much for him. He'd lined a box with blankets and food and had written a letter to them explaining that he was barely able to manage his own life, much less theirs. It was time for them to go back to the woods. He reread the letter. But he couldn't do it. He couldn't send them away. He balled up the piece of paper and threw it at the trash can. It bounced off the rim and rolled under his chair.

Dave sighed and put the box away in his closet. He opened the bedroom door to peek out at the sleeping chipmunks. They were adorable when they slept. But they weren't there. Or at least he couldn't see them on the foldout couch.

Dave checked under the couch. He called for them out the front door. He looked out the window. But the chipmunks didn't answer. They were gone.

* * *

The moonlight glowed through the windows of the California mansion. A sleepy man, wearing a kimono, was headed to bed. It was Ian, the music executive who had rejected Dave's songs. The doorbell rang. He paused on the winding staircase. Who could it be at this time of night?

Ian opened the door but no one was there.

When he went back inside he heard singing. Chipmunk singing. He looked down and saw the same chipmunks who had been silent the day before. Now they were singing Dave's Christmas song. Ian was stunned into silence.

"Looks like Christmas came early for you," chirped Alvin.

"Unless you'd like us to sing for a rival record company," added Simon.

Ian most definitely did not want that. It was a great holiday song, an unforgettable holiday song, and the chipmunks were unbelievable singers.

Ian smiled. This really *was* something new.

chapter 14

After searching most of the night for the chipmunks, Dave had finally fallen asleep on top of his bed fully dressed. It was the noise from a morning cartoon that woke him up. The television was on! Dave smiled, happy. The chipmunks were back!

He took them to the supermarket and gave them a lecture as they walked up and down the aisles.

"New rules," said Dave sternly. "No going out after nine, and not at all unless you tell me where you're going."

The chipmunks were all sitting in a child carrier strapped into Dave's shopping cart.

"You were worried about us, weren't you, Dave?"

"No," said Dave, looking away at the food on the shelves. "I need to know. That's all." He reached for an item and put it in the shopping cart.

Other shoppers in the grocery store stared at Dave and quickly moved away. He looked like some crazy person talking to himself.

"If you're not worried, then why—" asked Alvin.

"I need to know, okay?" interrupted Dave. It was hard to get them to listen sometimes.

Another shopper moved away as fast as she could. Dave grabbed some toaster waffles. *Bonk!* A tuna can bounced off his head.

"OW!" screamed Dave. He turned on the chipmunks. "You little . . . " Then he stopped. A little girl was sitting in a different shopping cart. Her mother, looking apologetic, was holding some cans. Dave handed her back the tuna. "Kids, huh?" He smiled.

"They keep you on your toes." The mother sighed. "You have any?"

"Three boys," said Dave, without a pause.

"Some days are better than others," the mother commented. She and Dave shared a little laugh.

"Yeah, and then some days you just want to close them in a box, and leave the box in a park and run away, you know?" Dave chuckled, remembering last night, but the mother's smile had faded away. She wheeled her daughter out of the aisle as fast as she could.

Dave returned to his shopping cart, and saw the chipmunks had filled it with toaster waffles.

Dave sighed and started putting toaster waffles back on the shelf.

"We can't afford all of these," he said. "In case you haven't noticed, I'm out of a job."

"Not our toaster waffles!" cried the chipmunks.

"*Ssh!*" whispered Dave. "Quiet down!" These chipmunks really needed to learn how to behave.

Just at that moment, a new song began to play over the grocery store loudspeakers. It was a familiar song. It was the chipmunks singing over the loudspeaker! And it was Dave's song! The chipmunks were singing his holiday song! Dave couldn't believe it. His jaw dropped open. The chipmunks were smiling up at him.

Dave's cell phone started ringing. He fumbled in his pocket, flipped it open, and heard Ian's voice. "Dave! My favorite songwriter!"

"Uh," mumbled Dave, flabbergasted. "Ian?"

"Tell me you heard the song!"

"I'm listening to it right now. But how did, I mean, *when* did . . . ?" He couldn't figure out what was going on. How did all this happen?

"Speed of business, baby," said Ian. "Got some friends in satellite radio. They immediately put it in heavy rotation. The video of your little guys has had ten million hits online already. It's crazy! Well, gotta run! Oh, and get them some clothes. It's embarrassing."

Dave stared at his phone before shutting it. The song was still playing over the loudspeaker. He was dumbfounded. He looked down at the chipmunks.

"We owed you, Dave," said Alvin.

chapter 15

All across America people were listening to the Chipmunks' holiday hit. Men and women would start humming the catchy tune, enjoying the high-pitched harmony, and then actually see the singers on TV and stop in their tracks wherever they were, completely shocked. These Chipmunks could sing! The Chipmunks starred on the covers of all the popular magazines. Even the science journals had articles about their amazing abilities. America was nuts for the Chipmunks!

The Chipmunks were everywhere. In her apartment, Claire put down the magazine she was reading, stunned and amazed. Dave *had* been telling the truth. She owed him an apology.

At home, Dave settled into caring for the little guys. He read them stories at night after he'd tucked them into the sleeper sofa. Every morning, he made them huge stacks of toaster waffles. They hung Christmas lights around the apartment in preparation for the holiday. And he made them sweaters to wear out of some of his old socks. He handed them to the chipmunks to try on.

"How come Alvin gets a letter?" Theodore pouted. Dave had sewn a big letter "A" across the front of one of the sweaters.

"Because he likes me better!" boasted Alvin.

"This reeks of favoritism, Dave," said Simon. He had been checking off the days until Christmas on a calendar, but now he was upset.

Dave let out a frustrated sigh.

"Do you like Alvin better?" asked Theodore in a tiny voice.

"No!" insisted Dave.

"Then how come he gets a letter?"

Dave rubbed his temples, exasperated. This was all so

complicated. He thought they'd like the sweaters. He thought they would make them all so happy. He'd had the idea for the letter at the last minute and didn't realize everyone had to have one. "I'm only one person, okay? And I've been a little busy writing songs and making tiny costumes!"

That night, when Dave was asleep, he felt someone next to him on his pillow. Little paws lifted Dave's eyelids. "Are you awake?" whispered Theodore.

"I am now," groaned Dave.

"Can I sleep with you?" Theodore asked, trembling. "I had a nightmare."

Dave hesitated.

"You won't even know I'm here," said Theodore.

Dave couldn't resist that adorable, terrified face. He pulled back the covers. "Sure. Just stay on that side of the bed."

"Okay!" agreed Theodore delightedly, and he instantly snuggled as close to Dave's arm as he could.

"Theodore," said Dave. "That's not your side of the bed."

But Theodore was already asleep and snoring.

The next morning, Theodore was sprawled across Dave's face when Alvin and Simon startled them awake bouncing on the bed up and down and screaming. "Wake up, Theodore! It's Christmas!"

Dave rubbed his eyes. He'd completely forgotten about Christmas. "Uh, yeah. Christmas. Great. I'm coming, I'm coming."

"Hurry up, Dad!" chirped Theodore.

Dave stopped short. "Dad?"

Theodore blushed from head to toe. "Dave. I said Dave," he whispered.

Dave brushed off what had just happened and walked out into the living room. A small Christmas tree was set up in the corner. The chipmunks were all racing around, too excited to sit still.

"Open mine first!" begged Theodore.

"No, mine first!" interrupted Alvin.

"No, mine!" said Simon.

"Wait," said Dave, stunned. "You guys got me presents?"

"Of course!" trilled the chipmunks together.

Dave looked uneasy, but Simon pushed forward and handed Dave a roughly wrapped present. Dave tore open the paper and looked at the small metal item inside it. He turned it over in his hand. "Wow!" He stalled for time, examining the present. "It's a . . . a . . . a . . ."

"Paper clip compass!" squealed Simon.

"A paper clip compass," repeated Dave, turning it over in his hand. "Exactly what I need. I will never get lost. Thank you, Simon."

"Me next!" said Alvin. He thrust his present toward Dave.

Dave opened it up carefully. It was a wallet. *His* wallet, actually. "Wow," said Dave finally. "It's my wallet."

"I wanted to get you something you use every day!" said Alvin.

"And I've been using this for almost ten years now. Very thoughtful, Alvin. Thank you."

Theodore came forward last of all. Shyly, he held up a large construction paper card. On it was a Magic

Marker drawing he had clearly done himself. "Very nicely done," commented Dave.

He opened the card. Inside were some writing and four balloonlike drawings. "Let me see. It says, 'Merry Christmas,' and it's got a picture of . . . of . . . of . . ." Dave hesitated, and then tried again. "Some pineapples?"

"Those aren't pineapples," said Theodore, shaking his head. He pointed at the card. "That's us. That's our family." He gave Dave a big, eager smile.

Dave patted Theodore stiffly on the head. He was embarrassed. It wasn't like he was their father or anything. After all, he wasn't even a chipmunk! He busied himself folding up their pajamas and putting away their pillows. "Look, fellas, let's make sure we understand one another. I'm not your dad or anything, right?"

"But you're like a dad!" chirped Theodore hopefully.

"No. Not really," said Dave, looking away. "I mean we're pals for sure, and I write your music and, you know, manage your career."

"Make us sweaters," added Simon.

"Feed us," chimed in Alvin.

"Let us sleep in your bed when we have nightmares," said Theodore.

All three chipmunks looked up at Dave with their round, brown eyes.

"That's what friends do. Okay?"

"Okay," said the chipmunks together, but they didn't look very happy. Tears were welling up in Theodore's eyes.

"Hey," said Dave, changing the subject. "Who wants to open presents?"

"Yeah!" cheered the chipmunks, instantly happy again.

Dave ran over to the counter and came back with three plain, white envelopes. He handed one to each chipmunk. They tore them open, but no one—not even Simon—knew what was inside them. Alvin turned over the piece of paper he'd found inside. It had a lot of writing on it.

"Savings bonds," explained Dave.

"It's money?" asked Alvin.

"It will be in seven years. You'll be able to buy something real nice for yourselves in seven years."

The chipmunks nodded their heads. They tried to be good sports.

"This is great, Dave," said Simon politely.

"Yeah, Dave," added Alvin.

"Thanks, Dave," said Theodore very quietly.

"So what else did you get us?" asked Alvin bravely.

Dave laughed nervously. "You'll see," he said. "Just wait here while your ol' pal Dave goes and gets them."

Dave hurried into the kitchen and began frantically searching the drawers and cupboards. He returned a few minutes later with three items crudely wrapped in paper towels.

"Okay!" blustered Dave. "Alvin, for you!" He handed him one of the "gifts."

Alvin tore off the paper and held up a rubber wine stopper with a pull handle. Alvin examined it very carefully. "What is it?" he asked politely.

"What is it?" repeated Dave, stalling for time. "It's a pogo stick! Go ahead. Give it a try!"

"Maybe later," Alvin coughed. "Wanted a guitar . . ."

Simon opened his and found a key chain ring with

an attached screwdriver nub.

"It's for all your keys!" exclaimed Dave.

"I don't have any keys," muttered Simon.

"Oh, well, it can also be used as a screwdriver," said Dave with fake cheer.

Next, Theodore slowly unwrapped the last gift with a look of dread on his face. He held up a worn dishcloth he'd seen a hundred times in the kitchen.

"It's a blanky!" explained Dave. "Guaranteed to keep all your nightmares away."

"It smells like old salad," whispered Theodore.

Dave knew he'd blown it. He felt terrible. He'd never bought presents for little kids before—much less chipmunks. Just then, the front door burst open.

"Ho, ho, ho! Who wants presents?" roared Ian, as he barged into the room, his arms loaded down with brightly wrapped gifts. "Bring them in, boys," he called, and workers came in carrying a battery-operated car just big enough for little chipmunks to drive on their own. As soon as the workers put the car on the ground, the chipmunks jumped in and started racing around the room.

"There's plenty more where those came from boys!" said Ian.

"Ian?" Dave asked. "What are you doing here?"

"Taking care of the talent, Dave. Taking care of the talent. What did you give them?"

"A bunch of junk from the kitchen," said Alvin, racing past in the car.

Ian smirked. "What every kid dreams of." Ian leaned against Dave's chair. "Don't worry about it. The important thing is that Uncle Ian came through for them." Realizing all of a sudden that he had actually touched something in Dave's apartment, Ian cleaned his hands with an antibacterial wipe.

"Uncle Ian?" questioned Dave.

"You know what else?" continued Ian. "Your Uncle Ian is putting together a big party to launch the new CD. Press, celebrities, hotshots, the whole nine yards."

"Cool!" squealed the chipmunks.

chapter 16

Limousines arrived at the hip dance club. Cameras flashed as celebrities walked up the red carpet. Fans rushed forward for autographs. It was the big party for the Chipmunks' first album—and all the cool people were there!

Inside the club, the dance music throbbed, and the beautiful people talked too loudly to make their voices heard. Claire was on assignment. A press pass dangled from her neck. She snapped photos of the stars.

Ian appeared and pushed his way through the crowd—shaking hands, high-fiving, and showing off how important he was. He made his way up to the stage and tapped the microphone. "Ladies and gentlemen," he crooned. "This is a very special night."

The crowd turned toward the stage. The talking stopped. Everyone was listening to Ian.

"At Jett Records we pride ourselves in discovering tomorrow's music today. And guess what? I did it again! Here they are! The Chipmunks!"

The lights blazed on the stage. The crowd applauded wildly. Two large doors swung open, and a gleaming car cruised up the red carpet. Dave and the Chipmunks were waving to the crowd from the open sunroof.

The car pulled to a stop, and the doors opened. Despite the glare from flashing cameras, Dave was able to make out Claire in the crowd. He struck a rock-star pose and made her laugh.

"Give it up, everyone, for the Chipmunks, playing their new hit single, 'Witch Doctor'!" bellowed Ian.

The crowd roared with applause as the Chipmunks appeared on top of a cauldron on the stage and burst into song. When they broke into their dance, everyone roared with delight.

Out in the audience, Claire was smiling and taking

lots of pictures—mostly of Dave. As the band hit the final note, she put her camera down to applaud with everyone else.

Later, when more photographers were snapping photos of Dave and the Chipmunks in front of a Jett Records backdrop, Claire came over. "Mind if I grab a few shots?"

"Claire!" exclaimed Dave, surprised to see her. "Not at all. Fire away."

Claire was taking photos of him from all different angles.

"So, how's it been going?" Dave asked her.

"Great," answered Claire. "I got a new assignment. I'm covering your rise to fame. Well, yours and . . ." Claire paused and smiled at the Chipmunks.

"Oh," said Dave. "This is Alvin, Simon, and Theodore. I forgot you guys never officially met."

"Hi," said Claire.

The chipmunks just blushed. Claire was very pretty. She tried to shake Alvin's paw, but he kissed her hand instead. Claire laughed.

"He's a flirt," said Dave. When Claire went to take more photos, Alvin held up bunny ears behind Theodore's head.

"Alvin, cut it out," Dave reprimanded him.

"So," said Claire. "I guess chipmunks aren't sabotaging your life anymore?"

"Nah. We have a pretty good arrangement."

"I'm sorry I didn't believe you that night. I really thought—"

"That I was insane?" finished Dave. "I understand. Talking chipmunks. It's a lot to take in over dinner."

"But look at you now. Got the career, a promising future . . ." Claire laughed shyly. "Kids. You're like a family."

"Don't say 'family' in front of Dave," chirped Alvin. "It gives him gas."

"It does not!"

"He doesn't want a family," explained Theodore, trying not to look sad.

"I never said that," insisted Dave.

"His emotional growth is stunted," said Simon.

"My emotional growth is fine, thank you," said Dave firmly. He scrambled to change the subject. He really needed a moment alone with Claire. "Why don't you guys go and play or raid the dessert table or something?"

"Very subtle, Dave," said Alvin.

"Yeah, we can take a hint," pouted Theodore.

"Who's hinting?" said Dave.

Claire bent over to talk to the chipmunks. Nothing they had said surprised her. "Don't take it personally, you guys. Dave's just got a little commitment phobia. Some people don't know a good thing when they've got it, right, Dave?" The smile on her face had vanished. Claire turned her back to him and made her way through the crowd away from them. Dave sighed. He'd missed his chance.

"Zero for two, big fella," said Alvin.

"Come on," interrupted Theodore. "Let's go find the dessert table!" The chipmunks walked away, leaving Dave standing by himself.

Ian appeared, grinning, and threw an arm around Dave. He held up an ugly plush toy. "What do you think of this?" beamed Ian.

"What is it?" asked Dave.

"It's Alvin!" exclaimed Ian, surprised Dave didn't get it.

"It looks nothing like Alvin," said Dave. Honestly, it didn't even look like a chipmunk.

"It's a prototype," explained Ian. "We'll sell a million of them. They're voice activated. Say something to it."

Embarrassed, Dave leaned toward the plush toy. "Hello, ugly little Alvin doll that looks nothing like Alvin."

Immediately, the toy began singing—in Spanish.

"That's just weird," said Dave.

"Dave, we've got to expand the 'Munks fan base," insisted Ian. "The music is but a means to the big money. I'm thinking of a fur clothing line. Their own perfume—*Chipmunk Heat.*"

"Ian!" shouted Dave protectively. "They're kids!"

"Kids?" Ian laughed. "They're rats! And they could make us both so rich if you'd only let me work with them!"

Dave started to back away from Ian, looking for the

chipmunks so he could bring them home and get them to bed. "Can't hear you, Ian," he said. "The music is very loud in here."

"You don't want to go against me," whispered Ian, as Dave disappeared into the crowd. He sneered. "Because I never lose."

Across the crowded room, Ian saw Alvin at the food table.

"Love the new song, Alv." The slippery words oozed out of him. He took a casual sip of his drink.

Ian stepped closer to Alvin and leaned over to whisper to him. "Alvin, you're a rock star. You should be traveling in limousines and private planes. Going to parties like this every night." He gestured toward the food table.

"Dave says we need our sleep," answered Alvin. Boy, that food table was amazing, though.

"So like Dave. So selfish," sighed Ian, shaking his head. "You'll sleep later when nobody is buying your records anymore."

Alvin looked startled, but Ian kept talking. "Which

is not going to happen," he soothed, "as long as I'm looking after you. Oh, Alvin, it hurts me to say this, but Dave's holding you back. I could be making you twenty large a day!"

Alvin's mouth dropped open. He was outraged! And then confused. "Is that a lot?" he asked Ian.

"Yes," hissed Ian. "And I didn't want to say this, but behind your back, Dave calls you 'the rats.'"

Now Alvin was devastated. How could Dave say such a thing? He made them breakfast, read them stories, tucked them in at night. Had it all been a game so he could make money off them? It was true that he hadn't gotten them Christmas presents like Ian. Alvin felt like he'd been punched in the stomach. He didn't know what to say.

But he didn't have to say anything. Ian was already talking again. "Now, me?" Ian was saying. "I consider you boys my family. You need anything, your Uncle Ian is there for you." He slipped a business card into Alvin's paw, gave him a wink, and slipped away into the crowd.

chapter 17

Simon was floating across the living room of the apartment. He'd turned a fan on, tied himself to a giant mylar balloon, and up, up, and away he'd gone. He whooped and hollered as he soared through the air. Until he saw that he was headed toward the sharp blades of the ceiling fan. Yikes! But he got caught in a new draft from that fan and drifted away—right to the open window. *"Alvin!"* he yelled at the top of his lungs.

But Alvin wasn't paying attention. He was parked in front of a video game system, pressing buttons furiously to shoot attackers. He was mesmerized. "Not now, Simon," he said, without looking away. "I'm about to hit a triple body count."

"Heeeeelllppp!" screamed Simon. The open window loomed closer. Simon kicked his legs as hard as he could, trying to "swim" backward through the air, but it didn't do any good. He tried to grab onto the window frame, but his arms were too short. He was headed out into the sky above Los Angeles.

"Hey, guys, I've got a new song for you," Dave said, as he came into the room. He stopped when he saw Simon, rushed over, and grabbed him at the very last moment. He slammed the window shut and left Simon floating in midair so he could look right into his eyes.

"Hey, Dave," said Simon.

"What's going on in here?" demanded Dave. He looked around at the mess and shook his head. "I thought I told you guys to clean up around here."

"We are," said Alvin.

A very pretty cleaning woman walked out of the bathroom, a bucket in her hand.

"Who's that?" asked Dave, startled.

"Uncle Ian hired us a housekeeper," said Alvin. "She's also a supermodel." He went back to banging at the controller of his video game. "I had four extra grenades!" he yelled at it.

Now Dave noticed the screen. Something was exploding. "Where did you get that game?" demanded Dave, horrified at how violent it was.

"Uncle Ian," said Alvin, without looking up. He started screaming at the screen. "How am I supposed to kill the trolls without a grenade?"

"That's enough," said Dave sternly. He clicked off the television.

"Hey! I was on the final alien planet!" exclaimed Alvin.

"Where's Theodore?" asked Dave. He heard some noises from the kitchen. He ran in and discovered Theodore on the counter beside an enormous gift basket sent by Ian, stuffing an entire box of candy into his mouth. His cheeks were all puffed out with what looked like little basketballs.

"Spit it out!" Dave ordered.

Theodore shook his head and then swallowed hard.

"All right! That's it!" yelled Dave. "In the living room! Everybody! NOW!"

Dave asked the housekeeper to leave them alone and assembled the chipmunks on the couch. It was time for a family meeting.

"It's hard. I know it's hard," began Dave. "A few months ago you were, I don't know, hanging out in a tree somewhere, and now you're—"

"Major rock stars," interrupted Alvin.

"Whatever," said Dave. "The point is just because you're—"

"Major rock stars," interrupted Alvin again.

"Okay. But that doesn't mean you can do whatever you want."

"Uncle Ian says we should always be happy," said Simon.

How would he explain this to them? Dave took a breath. "First of all, he's not your uncle."

"He also says we should be making almost twenty dollars a day!" said Alvin, remembering his conversation with Ian from the other night. He wanted to get back to his video game. He was sure he could blast away that troll this time.

"You're making way more than that," said Dave. "But I'm putting it away for you. You know, like storing nuts for the winter."

"Winter is for losers!" said Alvin.

"And shouldn't we have a say about building a proper investment portfolio?" questioned Simon. He adjusted his glasses.

Dave stared at his little chipmunks lined up on the couch. What had happened to them? They used to be so innocent, so sweet. "Where is all this coming from?" he demanded. "You're just kids."

"Kids, Dave?" asked Alvin pointedly. "Or rats?"

"What?"

Theodore chimed in. "Uncle Ian says we're like his family."

After all he'd done for them, Dave couldn't believe this. Okay, he'd messed up Christmas, but what about the meals he'd cooked, the messes he'd cleaned up? "Oh yeah," he said, losing his temper. "You love Uncle Ian so much, you think I'm not watching out for you guys—fine. Why don't you live with *him*?"

But those weren't the words that Theodore wanted to hear. Not at all. He was stunned into silence. And so were Simon and Alvin. It was true, what Ian had said: Dave really didn't love them.

chapter 18

The chipmunks huddled together in a dark corner of the closet with a flashlight. They were voting on what they would do next. Was it time to stop living with Dave? Alvin pulled out a scrap of paper from a hat. "One vote yes," he read. He pulled out another piece of paper. "Two votes yes."

Alvin went to draw out the last vote, but there wasn't one. The hat was empty. "We have a problem with voter turnout," he said.

"Theodore," said Simon accusingly.

But Theodore wasn't ready to make a decision. He wasn't ready to give up on Dave. For so long, he'd wanted Dave to be his dad, and he thought of him that way. "I want to talk to Dave first," he said to his two brothers.

Alvin and Simon were exasperated, but what could they do? They waited in the closet while Theodore went to Dave's room.

The bedroom was dark, lit only by the moon. Dave was asleep. On his way across the floor, Theodore saw a crumpled up piece of paper under the chair. Theodore picked it up, smoothed it, and read it by the moonlight.

It was the long-ago letter Dave had written the chipmunks, telling them he wanted them to go back to the woods. It was the letter Dave couldn't send. But Theodore didn't know that. For all he knew, Dave had written it that very night. Theodore's eyes watered as he read it, and a tear rolled down his striped cheek. He sniffled, trying not to cry. He loved Dave so much, but it was over. It was really over.

chapter 19

A big black SUV pulled up in front of Dave's apartment. The chipmunks had already crawled inside and buckled up. Dave stood on the curb watching as the chauffeur picked up their suitcases and put them in the back.

Ian rolled down his tinted window. "I told you, Dave, I never lose."

The limo pulled away, leaving Dave alone by the side of the road.

When they got to Ian's mansion, the chipmunks couldn't believe it. It was like an amusement park that had been created just for them. A sign that said WELCOME HOME, CHIPMUNKS! was draped across the center of the main room, and there were toys everywhere. Lots and lots of toys.

"Wow!" exclaimed the chipmunks together.

Theodore was awed. "Can we play with all this stuff?" he asked.

"Why not?" snickered Ian. "This is your house."

"What are the rules?" asked Simon.

"I have only one rule," explained Ian slowly, saying each word carefully. "There are no rules."

The chipmunks cheered.

"Go to bed when you want," said Ian. "Wake up when you want. Eat what you want. Uncle Ian just wants you to be happy."

The chipmunks charged into the mansion and dived into the pile of toys.

All day long, they played and played. At one point out on the tennis courts, Simon crawled into the air cannon used for automatically serving balls. A butler adjusted the cannon exactly the way Simon told him to, and the he fired it. *Wham!* Simon shot through the air and landed with a tiny splash in the swimming pool.

Alvin, Theodore, and Ian, all lounging in deck chairs, held up judge's cards.

Later, Alvin found a trampoline and started doing flips.

"Playing hard?" Ian asked, when he walked through.

"Yup," said Alvin, as he flew through the air.

"Good," continued Ian. " 'Cause tomorrow we start working hard. Coast-to-coast in five days."

Theodore had tumbled into the room while he was talking. "Dave says that touring is no life for a kid."

"No life for a *normal* kid," answered Ian. "But you guys are superstars! Which reminds me, Simon. Let's get rid of those lame glasses." Ian plucked Simon's glasses from his head, broke them in half, and replaced them with a superhip, supercool new pair.

"These would be great," protested Simon. "Unless I needed them to see." He walked into a wall.

"Your eyes will adjust," said Ian. "Let's hit the road, boys!"

The chipmunks were thrilled. They were going on the road—just like real rock stars!

chapter 20

The Rabid Transit Tour had begun! Every night was a new city and another concert. In Austin, the audience went wild. In New Orleans, the audience wanted an encore. In New York City, the show sold out! The Chipmunks were bigger stars than ever!

Flash! Flash! Cameras snapped pictures of them everywhere they went. It was exhausting. During a photo shoot for a magazine, little Theodore just couldn't stay awake. He couldn't even remember what city he was in. Every time the famous photographer went to take his picture, his eyes would shut. Irritated, the photographer shook his head. Simon tried to prop Theodore awake. Ian brought over a plate of toaster waffles. They could have the waffles when they smiled.

Later, the chipmunks had to shoot a commercial for pet food, and they were even more tired. They sat at a kitchen table in front of bowls of kibble. A big bag of Perky Pet Food was on the table. But the chipmunks weren't perky. They couldn't stop yawning.

The director called, "Action!" They were supposed to start eating the food, but Theodore had fallen asleep, and his head landed in his bowl with a thud. The director threw up his hands. This time, Ian pulled out a big horn and blasted it in Theodore's ears. That woke him up.

At the recording studio, however, Theodore could hardly stand up. All the chipmunks leaned against one another, trying to remember the words to their new song, trying not to yawn into the microphone.

"Hold it!" yelled the recording engineer.

Ian screamed at the engineer in the sound booth. The engineer pointed at the chipmunks and yelled back at him. Suddenly, Ian had an idea. He pulled out his cell phone and made a quick call.

"Here, boys," he said a few minutes later. He was carrying cardboard tray with four supersized paper cups. "Guess what Uncle Ian bought you—coffee!"

"Toffee?" asked Theodore, hopeful. "I love toffee!"

"Coffee, Theo. It's like an energy health drink," Ian explained. "With caramel and whipped cream and two pumps of chocolate syrup."

The chipmunks slurped down their drinks in under a minute.

"That ought to keep them awake," Ian said to the engineer, when he was back in the sound booth. He plopped down in a chair and sighed. He was making so much money these days.

But the coffee gave the chipmunks too much energy. Suddenly, *wham!* Alvin slammed against the glass wall of the sound booth. His eyes were practically popping out of his head. With a crazed look, he leaped onto on the mike boom and swung it around and around.

Whoosh! Simon flew by. He was running around the room as if it were a racetrack, hitting the walls as he went.

Boing! Boing! Boing! Theodore had a pogo stick and was jumping across the studio floor. It was chaos! It was too much coffee! The Chipmunks were completely out of control! They sang three times faster than normal and crashed to the floor at the end of the song. Ian shook his head and covered his eyes.

Back in LA, alone in his apartment, Dave didn't know what was happening with the chipmunks on the road. He felt lost and sad. One day, after he pulled down the sun visor in his car, three sticky, moldy toaster waffles slid into his lap. He missed the little guys.

Sometimes, Claire saw him through his apartment window just sitting in his living room, tossing Simon's paper airplane into the air and watching it loop back and forth across the room.

One night, Dave wandered into his kitchen. As he went to open the fridge, he saw Theodore's Christmas card with the stick figures of them all stuck to the door with a magnet. Dave pulled it off and opened it. He looked longingly at the "pineapple" family—he missed the chipmunks so much.

chapter 21

The Chipmunks were getting ready for a concert rehearsal. Dancers were onstage warming up. The wind machine was blowing. Dry ice was making fog rise in the air while Ian was checking out the Chipmunks' new costumes. He gave them a once-over. "I love it," he decided.

"We don't," said Alvin, mad.

Instead of their usual sweaters, the chipmunks were wearing gaudy costumes made from spandex, sparkles, and leather. Their fur had been slicked back with gel. They were even wearing eyeliner.

"I feel like a girl raccoon," said Alvin when he saw Ian.

"And the new songs don't sound like 'us,'" added Simon.

"'Us'?" mocked Ian. "I'm 'us,' too. And I think the new direction is perfect. It's all about edge."

"Dave always said it was all about the music," insisted Alvin.

"Yeah?" said Ian. "Well, Dave isn't here, okay. Now let's rehearse! We've got a show tomorrow! Take it four beats from the top. Go!"

A girl dance troupe stepped out onstage and posed behind the Chipmunks. The wind machines were blowing, the dancers were kicking up their legs, the color wheels were spinning, the dry ice was making fog, and the Chipmunks looked exhausted. Theodore began to cough.

Ian was furious. He stopped the act. He was just demanding more dry ice when his cell phone rang. "Hello!" he answered cheerily. But then his smile evaporated. It was the last person in the whole world that he wanted to talk to. It was Dave.

"Dave Seville," said Ian with fake warmth. "How's

my favorite songwriter?"

Dave paced back and forth in his living room while he talked to Ian. He'd been getting more and more worried about the chipmunks. "Just let me talk to the guys," he said to Ian.

"I don't think that's such a good idea," said Ian. "My boys are still stinging since you kicked them out the door."

"That's not what happened," protested Dave.

"De-ni-al," said Ian, drawing out each syllable of the word.

Dave changed the subject. "So what's this I hear about a European tour? You're taking them away for six months?"

"Twelve," corrected Ian, "if I can get China to go Chipmunk."

"Look," begged Dave. "I just wanted to say hi, see how they're doing."

Ian glanced at the stage where the tired Chipmunks were dragging themselves through another number. "I can answer that," he said. "They're doing great. Lovin' life. They've moved on, Dave, and they're happy. They're really, really happy."

"I'm really, really happy, too," said Dave defensively.

"I'm not surprised," said Ian. "See? This worked out for everyone."

"Just let me talk to them," Dave pleaded.

Ian stifled a yawn. "Wish I could, Dave. But we're finishing up our U.S. tour tomorrow night, and they don't need the stress. We'll send you a postcard."

"Ian, I'm going to see them!"

"Hello? Hello?" said Ian, pretending not to hear. He clicked shut his phone. The chipmunks were staring at him.

"Was that Dave?" chirped Alvin.

"Yeah," said Ian. "He just called to say how great he's doing. He's really, really happy."

"Is he coming to the show?" asked Simon.

Ian shook his head. "I sent him tickets, but he's sent them back. Sorry, guys. I guess he's got better things to do."

The chipmunks looked so disappointed. Theodore tried not to cry.

"Hey, why the long furry faces?" said Ian cheerfully. "We've got a show to prepare for! This is gonna be fun! Everybody back to work!"

The smoke machines started up again. The dancers began kicking. Simon tried to keep up. Meanwhile, Ian took a moment to whisper some instructions to a security guard. "Dave Seville," he said slowly. "Learn the name, look for the face. If he shows up here tomorrow night, he gets nowhere near my chipmunks. Got it?"

chapter 22

Theodore padded across the cold marble floor of the hallway. It was so dark in the mansion at night. He scurried into Ian's bedroom and climbed up onto the bed where Ian was fast asleep.

"Ahhh!" shouted Ian, rolling over and finding himself face to face with a chipmunk. "What are you doing here?"

"Can I sleep with you?" begged Theodore, trembling. "I had a nightmare."

Ian groaned. Was that all? "I had a nightmare, too," he said to Theodore. "I had a nightmare that I had to throw together thirty-seven concerts in sixteen countries, and I had to coordinate radio and print interviews in five different languages."

Theodore blinked at him. That just didn't sound as scary as his nightmare.

"But the difference is," continued Ian, glaring at him, "that when I open my eyes, the nightmare doesn't end." Ian picked up the little chipmunk and hurled him out into the hall. Then he slammed the bedroom door shut.

Terrified to be alone again in Ian's vast cold mansion, Theodore huddled in a sliver of moonlight. He reached up inside of his sweater and pulled out the dirty dishcloth Dave had given him for Christmas. It had obviously been held and folded again and again. Theodore held it close like a blanket. It was the only thing that comforted him anymore.

In another room of the mansion, Simon was repairing a pair of glasses. They were the ones that Ian had taken from him and tossed aside when they'd first arrived. Simon wrapped a last piece of tape around the glasses and put them on. Ah! The world wasn't blurry anymore! He could see again. He liked these glasses so much better than the fancy ones Ian had given him. He decided to go find Alvin.

Alvin was up on the roof looking up at the stars. In his hands was the harmonica he'd found at Dave's on their first day at his apartment. He raised it to his lips now and blew a few sad notes. Simon came out onto the roof and sat beside him. Together, they looked out across the silence of the night. A few minutes later, Theodore crawled over to them and snuggled close.

"I want to go home," he whispered.

"You are home," said Simon.

"No," disagreed Theodore. "*Home* home. With Dave."

Alvin sighed. "Theodore, wake up and smell the toffee. Dave doesn't want us. If he cared about us, he'd at least come to the show."

Alvin didn't know that Dave had really wanted to see them. Theodore began to hum a sad and lonely song. Simon joined in, and Alvin sang harmony. Their high, sweet voices drifted into the night air.

chapter 23

Ian was pacing back and forth outside the dressing rooms of the Orpheum Theater. The kickoff for their European tour was tonight. Boxes of Chipmunk merchandise—toys, mugs, T-shirts—littered the hallway. Ian looked at his watch. Why weren't they ready? The show had to start!

Inside the dressing room, a vet was examining each of the chipmunks in turn. Alvin tried to sing a simple scale, but his voice was too raspy. So was Simon's. Theodore couldn't hit a single note.

The vet looked down Alvin's throat with a tongue depressor. "You three sound like you've been gargling nails."

A few minutes later, the vet emerged from the dressing room, shaking her head.

"Well?" asked Ian eagerly.

"I could give you a lot of fancy terms," said the vet. "But, bottom line, they're exhausted."

"Can't you give them a shot or something?" Ian urged. "I've invested every dime I've got in these guys."

The vet looked at Ian with distaste. "They need a long rest," she said sternly.

"A long rest," repeated Ian, snickering. "Right." He guided the vet away from the dressing rooms. He needed to get rid of this meddlesome busybody. "Good call," he told her sarcastically. "I'll take care of it. They're like my own kids, you know. Thank you so much, doctor. Really appreciate it."

Ian grabbed a toy Chipmunk out of a crate. "Chipmunk-fever," he said. "Catch it." He threw the plush toy at the vet. She caught it and shook her head. Ian slipped into the dressing room.

The Chipmunks were all lying down, exhausted. They sounded like they had laryngitis. They had just been going too hard, singing too much.

"Guys," began Ian. "I've been doing a lot of soul searching—yes, I have a soul—and I just don't feel right about sending you out there like this."

"You're canceling the show?" asked Theodore.

"Of course not!" said Ian, horrified. "That means refunds. And your Uncle Ian is allergic to refunds. I'm talking about having you lip-synch the songs."

Simon wrinkled up his forehead. "Isn't that like cheating?"

"No!" blustered Ian. "It's more like . . . helping. All the big stars do it. You just have to make sure to mouth the words exactly the way we recorded it. Otherwise, people will know . . ."

"I don't want to do it," said Simon.

"Me neither!" said Theodore.

"I will," said Alvin. His brothers looked shocked.

"What's the big deal?" protested Alvin. "We're superstars. No one will ever know."

Ian grinned. "That's why he's the one with the big yellow 'A.'"

Outside the theater, the parking lots were full of cars, and fans were streaming in from all directions. Dave ran as fast as he could through the crowd up to the ticket booth, but the moment the ticket seller saw him, she slapped up a sign that said SOLD OUT.

"Aw, come on!" exclaimed Dave, trying to catch his breath. "You don't have one more ticket?"

But the ticket seller only shrugged and closed the window.

Dave tried to run inside, but a security guard grabbed Dave by the elbow.

"I have to get in," Dave protested. "I'm Dave Seville. The Chipmunks used to be my band. You know—" He started to hum their first hit.

The guard wasn't listening. He tried to steer Dave back toward the parking lot.

"Oh, I get it. It's sold out for *me*." Dave shook himself loose. "Don't need to draw me a diagram. You don't want me here, fine. I'm gone." He played it cool and backed away, keeping an eye on the security guard. Then he dashed around the corner to a side entrance to the theater.

Dave approached the press coordinator, the person who managed all the reporters and photographers. He gave her his name, but she couldn't find it on her list.

"That's impossible!" said Dave, pretending to be insulted. "I'm the editor of the, uh, *LA Music Journal*. Could you check again?"

When the coordinator began peering at her sheet again, Dave tried to sneak inside. But the coordinator was too quick for him. She grabbed him at the last moment. It was all over. He wouldn't see the chipmunks for more than a year.

But then another hand took his arm and pulled him aside. "He's with me," someone said to the coordinator. It was Claire, her camera and press pass dangling from around her neck. Together, they rushed into the theater's lobby.

"What's going on?" asked Claire.

Seeing security everywhere, Dave pulled Claire under a stairwell. "I've got to get my boys back," he said urgently. "But Ian's trying to keep me out."

"Your *boys*?" questioned Claire, smiling.

"Yeah, I know that must sound really weird coming from me."

"It's a good weird," said Claire happily.

"Not a great weird?" asked Dave. Claire burst out laughing. "'Cause after all I did to mess up everything, you included, I don't want to settle for just 'good.'"

"Dave, the boys. We should go."

"Right." He took Claire's hand, and together they ran toward the theater doors.

Onstage, the Chipmunks took their places in the dark. They were supposed to look like tough-guy rappers. The stage lights blazed into their eyes. The music blasted on, and Alvin grabbed the microphone. He lip-synched perfectly. Simon and Theodore strutted awkwardly behind him.

The enormous crowd cheered. They raised their arms and began swaying back and forth just like they did at every concert. The Chipmunks starred on enormous screens on both sides of the stage.

Simon and Theodore couldn't believe that Alvin was

lip-synching. But they had no other choice. Their voices were gone. They began miming the words, too.

Claire and Dave made it to the back of the theater. Dave was stunned. He couldn't believe the outfits. He couldn't believe the music. And the dancing was horrible. "That is just so wrong," he said, shaking his head.

Claire was looking around at the audience. She saw security guards everywhere. "If you're going to do something, do it fast." She thought for a moment and took her camera and gave it to Dave. "Take this. You're press, remember?"

Dave started to leave. "It'll work better if you take this off," Claire said as she took off the lens cap.

Dave smiled gratefully and began pretending to snap photos as he headed down the aisle toward the stage.

Fans were screaming all around him, but he was getting closer—until a security guard noticed his face. Realizing at once who it was, the security guard urgently called Ian on his walkie-talkie.

Ian excused himself from the VIP lounge where he had been hanging out with celebrities and hurried toward the stage where the Chipmunks were still pretending to sing.

Alerted by Ian, all the security guards in the theater began to close in on Dave from different directions.

David could see them coming. He knew he had only seconds to act. He raised a hand to his mouth and yelled as loud as he could, at the top of his lungs, "ALVIN!"

But Alvin didn't hear him above the blaring music and the screaming fans.

A guard jumped on Dave and wrestled him to the ground. It was over. Now he'd never get to see them.

Backstage, Ian got the news on his walkie-talkie that Dave had been caught. He relaxed. Mission accomplished. "When is he going to learn?" Ian smiled to himself. He never lost.

chapter 24

Onstage, the Chipmunks continued their show, unaware that Dave had been in the audience. A teenage girl shrieked, "I love you, Alvin!"

Alvin pulled off the ridiculous outfit Ian had made him wear and tossed it into the crowd. Simon and Theodore were stunned. "Alvin, have you lost it?" asked Simon.

Alvin gave his brothers a mischievous wink. He wasn't done yet. He'd had a plan. He spun around in an elaborate dance move, dropped to his knees, and, just like that, stopped mouthing the words to the song.

Simon and Theodore spun around just like Alvin, dropped to their knees, and stopped moving their lips, too.

The Chipmunks' prerecorded voices kept on singing, but the audience was stunned. Theodore and Simon tossed their outfits into the crowd. They were chipmunks again!

Dave heard the crowd gasp as the security guards muscled him toward the exit. He turned to see the Chipmunks' rebellion against Ian.

"Liking this a lot," said Dave. He started laughing out loud. The Chipmunks knew better. They knew this act was ridiculous.

Claire used her other camera to capture it all on film—the stunned fans, the triumphant Chipmunks. They were goofing around now—playing air guitar and jumping on the drums and keyboards. They just needed to have fun again.

Some people in the audience booed. But a lot of other people were laughing at the Chipmunk silliness. In the midst of the commotion, Dave managed to wriggle free from the guards and disappear into the crowd. He got as close as he could to the stage again and began calling their names in a loud voice. This time, they heard him.

"Dave!" screamed Theodore.

"He's here!" shouted a delighted Simon.

"He is . . . ?" Alvin peered into the crowd.

Dave waved his hands, trying to get their attention. "Come on! I'm taking you home!"

"H-h-home?" stuttered Alvin. He was too excited to say anything else.

A security guard was closing in. There was no time to lose. The three chipmunks dashed toward the front of the stage and leaped through the air toward Dave's waiting arms—but before they could reach them, the velvet curtain crashed down.

Wham! The chipmunks hit the curtain with a defeated thud. But they weren't down for long. Three security guards approached, and the chipmunks scrambled up and began running away. One security guard tried to corner Theodore.

"I'll bite you!" he warned. "And I haven't had my rabies shot!" He bared his little teeth and started trying to growl.

The second guard tried to grab Simon but kept missing. "With your reflexes," said Simon, stepping out of his way, "might I suggest a desk job?"

The third guard zigzagged after Alvin, who taunted him. "Come on, man," he said. "You're better than this!" The guard lunged after him but caught only empty air.

The lumbering goons had no chance against the speedy chipmunks scurrying this way and that. But they stopped when they saw Dave appear behind the curtain. "Dave!" squealed Alvin.

"Guys!" yelled Dave in response. He charged forward, but the guards had a much easier time grabbing him.

Meanwhile, Ian had effortlessly caught the chipmunks by their tails and tossed them into a plastic-covered cat carrier. He slammed the caged door shut. "Better work on your French," he sneered. "We're leaving for Paris tonight."

Ian handed the carrier to a guard. The chipmunks pressed their faces to the bars and watched as Dave was dragged away by security. They were heartbroken.

The guard carried the chipmunks away from the stage. He put it on the floor of the hallway outside the dressing rooms. Alvin squeezed himself against the bars when the guard was gone. "You'll never take us alive!" he yelled.

"Sit down, Alvin," sighed Simon.

Backstage, Dave pleaded with Ian. "They don't want to do this anymore, Ian. Just let them go."

"Okay," said Ian. He laughed sarcastically.

"After tonight, they'll be booed everywhere they go."

Ian knocked on Dave's forehead. "*They're chipmunks that talk*. People will come."

Ian walked off with his security guards, only to return a moment later. He passed by Dave with a pet carrier and climbed into his stretch limousine.

Dave was ready to chase down the car on foot when Claire stopped him. "Dave!" she yelled.

"Ian's got the guys!" wailed Dave. "I'm not letting them get on that plane."

Together, they ran to Dave's car. Dave hit the gas as the limousine pulled out of the parking lot. "Step on it, Dave! You're losing them!" chirped a little voice. It was Alvin!

Dave and Claire whipped their heads around. Alvin, Simon, and Theodore were all sitting in the backseat, big grins on their faces. The car skidded to a stop.

Dave was incredibly happy, but confused. "How did you guys . . . ?" he wondered.

Simon pulled out the key chain Dave had given him for Christmas. He gave a Dave a sly smile. "You were right. It's also a screwdriver that works on locks," he reminded Dave.

Dave was amazed. They were always surprising him.

"You came back for us," chirped Theodore.

"Hey," said Dave. "We're a family. We've got to stick together."

The chipmunks and Claire exchanged expressions of mock surprise. Could this be Dave? Had he really said it?

"What?" said Dave, looking at them all.

"You just said the 'f' word!" exclaimed Alvin.

"Someone call a doctor!" said Simon.

"Do you need to lie down?" asked Claire.

"No, I'm good," smiled Dave. "Actually, I'm great!" He put the car into gear and began to drive. Almost instantly, the chipmunks began pestering him.

"Can I beep the horn?" begged Alvin.

"I want to beep it!" said Simon.

"Me, me! Let me beep it!" pleaded Simon.

Dave grinned at Claire. Families. This is just what they were like. And he let all the chipmunks clamber into the front seat and start beeping away.

chapter 25

The chipmunks were making a mess in the kitchen. Syrup was spilled on the counter, and burned waffles were flying through the air. It was just like old times.

Dave scanned the familiar scene as he came into the room. "Toaster waffles. Not just for breakfast anymore, eh, guys?"

The next waffle shot out of the toaster. "I got it! I got it!" yelled Simon, circling underneath it with his outstretched paws.

"A little more to the left," directed Dave.

"I can see, Dave!" said Simon, irritated. "I got it!"

Bonk! The waffle hit him directly between the eyes and knocked him over. Dave laughed, picked up the waffle, and put it on a plate. He slid it in front of Theodore, who slapped a dollop of whipped cream on top. Alvin poured on the syrup.

Dave went to grab another plate for the next incoming waffle and noticed that there were five of them put out instead of four. "Why are there five plates out?" he asked.

The doorbell rang before the chipmunks could answer—and it was Claire. Dave could see her through the glass of the front door. The chipmunks tried to look innocent, but Dave knew exactly what they were up to.

"I wonder who that could be?" asked Alvin with wide eyes.

Dave shook his head and went to open the door. "Claire," he said. She had never looked lovelier.

"Dave."

A steamy pop hit blasted over the music system, and Claire laughed out loud. "They're playing our song."

"I hope you like toaster waffles."

"And champagne!" announced Alvin.

On the counter near the table, Alvin straddled the

bottle, struggling to pull out the champagne cork. He heaved as hard as he could, and the cork popped out like a rocket, just missing Dave and Claire and crashing through the window.

"I'm not going to say it," muttered Dave, shaking his head.

Alvin fell forward from the effort of opening the bottle, grabbed the bottle, and flipped it out of the bucket onto the floor. Champagne and broken glass were everywhere.

Claire giggled. "Not going to say it?"

"Nope," said Dave, smiling. But at that exact moment, the spilled champagne seeped into a power strip on the floor sending sparks flying everywhere. A moment later, all the lights went out.

"ALVINNNN!"

epilogue

Ian had sat smugly in the limousine as it sped away from the theater. The carrier was by his side on the seat. "Tell you what," he told the Chipmunks. "If you guys behave yourselves, I'll let you call me Uncle Ian again. Deal?"

From inside the cage, three mechanical voices began speaking at once. "*Hola! Me llamo* Alvin!" "*Hola! Me llamo* Theodore!" "*Hola! Me llamo* Simon!"

Ian's eyes went wide. Since when did the chipmunks know Spanish? He whipped open the cage door and saw three talking Chipmunk dolls. He'd been fooled! He hadn't won after all! He was ruined. "Noooo!!!" he screamed.

Months later, he moved into his new office—a run-down dump in a bad section of town. He kept trying to find another act. "Sing! I said sing!" Ian yelled, as he pounded the keys of a broken piano.

Sitting on top of the piano were three very confused and frightened squirrels. They didn't know what the crazy man was saying. They didn't even know how to talk.

And they certainly didn't know how to sing like Dave Seville's famous Chipmunks.